Outside the glass was a strange world of bright, moving colour.

It looked like another planet.

The mini-sub was moving past red, yellow and blue coral – past little coral mountains, valleys and caves – past fishes of every colour and size.

"Can't we stay for a little bit? The answer to Morgan's riddle must be here somewhere," said Annie.

Jack nodded slowly. She might be right, he thought. Besides, when would they ever get a chance to visit a place like this again?

www.kidsatrandomhouse.co.uk

Read all the adventures of
Jack and *Annie*!

Magic Tree House™

DIVING with DOLPHINS!

MARY POPE OSBORNE

Illustrated by Philippe Masson

RED FOX

DIVING WITH DOLPHINS

A RED FOX BOOK 978 1 78295 387 6

Published in Great Britain by Red Fox,
an imprint of Random House Children's Publishers UK
A Random House Group Company

Published in the US, as *Dolphins at Daybreak*,
by Random House Children's Books, a division of Random House Inc, 1997

Red Fox edition published 2009

The Random House Group Limited supports the Forest Stewardship Council®
(FSC®), the leading international forest-certification organisation. Our books
carrying the FSC label are printed on FSC®-certified paper. FSC is the only
forest-certification scheme supported by the leading environmental
organisations, including Greenpeace. Our paper procurement policy can be
found at www.randomhouse.co.uk/environment

MIX
Paper from
responsible sources
FSC® C016897

Set in 16/21pt Bembo MT Schoolbook by
Falcon Oast Graphic Art Ltd.

Red Fox Books are published by Random House Children's Publishers UK,
61–63 Uxbridge Road, London W5 5SA

www.**kids**at**randomhouse**.com
www.**randomhouse**.co.uk

Addresses for companies within The Random House Group Limited can be found
at: www.randomhouse.co.uk/offices.htm

THE RANDOM HOUSE GROUP Limited Reg. No. 954009

A CIP catalogue record for this book is available from the British Library.

Printed and bound by CPI Group (UK) Ltd, Croydon, CR0 4YY

For Mattie Stepanek

Dear Reader,

While I was trying to decide what to do for book number nine, kids kept asking me to send Jack and Annie under the ocean.

"But how will they breathe and talk underwater?" I asked

After a number of kids suggested a submarine, I began researching the subject and learned about mini-subs, and that settled it.

So thanks to all the kids who've helped me – and keep helping me. I feel as if we're having these adventures together – you, me, Jack and Annie.

Where do we go next? And what do you think will happen when we get there? Let me know . . .

Mary Pope Osbourne

Contents

1

Master Librarians

Jack stared out of the kitchen window.

The sun was not up yet. But the sky was growing lighter.

Jack had been awake for a long time. He had been thinking about the dream he'd had – the dream about Morgan le Fay.

"The tree house is back", Morgan had said. "I'm waiting."

Jack wished that dreams were real. He missed Morgan's magic tree house.

"Jack!" His little sister Annie appeared

in the doorway. "We have to go to the woods *now*!" she said.

"Why?" Jack asked.

"I had a dream about Morgan!" exclaimed Annie. "She said the tree house is back and she's waiting for us!"

"That was *my* dream," said Jack.

"Oh, wow," said Annie. "She told you, too? So it *must* be important."

"But dreams aren't real," said Jack.

"Some dreams aren't. But this one is," said Annie. "I can feel it.' She opened the back door. "I'll see you later!"

"Wait – wait. I'm coming!' said Jack.

He raced up the stairs. Having the same dream must mean something, he thought.

He grabbed his rucksack and threw his notebook and pencil into it.

Then he ran downstairs.

"We'll be back soon, Mum," Jack called into the living room.

"Where you going so early?" his dad asked.

"Just for a quick walk!" said Jack.

"It rained last night," called his mum "Don't get your shoes wet."

"We won't!"

Jack slipped out of the door. Annie was waiting for him.

"Let's go!" she said.

The sky was pale grey. The air felt freshly washed.

Jack and Annie ran up their quiet street to the Frog Valley woods.

They headed between the trees. Soon they came to the tallest oak in the woods. There was a wooden house high in the treetop.

"It *is* back!" whispered Jack.

Someone looked out of the window of the tree house – a lovely old woman with long white hair. Morgan le Fay.

"Come up," called the magical librarian.

Jack and Annie climbed up the rope ladder and into the tree house.

In the dawn light, they stared at Morgan le Fay. She looked beautiful in a red velvet robe.

Jack pushed his glasses into place. He couldn't stop smiling.

"We both had dreams about you!" said Annie.

"I know," said Morgan.

"You do?"

"Yes, I sent them to you," Morgan told them, "because I need your help."

"What kind of help?" said Jack.

"Merlin the Magician has been up to his tricks again," said Morgan. "So I haven't had any time to collect books for Camelot's library."

"Can we collect them for you?" asked Annie.

"Yes, but in order to gather books through time you must be Master Librarians," said Morgan.

"Oh, well," Annie said sadly.

"But you can *become* Master

Librarians," said Morgan, "if you pass the test."

"Really?" said Annie.

"What kind of test?" Jack asked.

"You must show that you know how to do research," said Morgan, "and show that you can find answers to hard questions."

"How?" asked Annie.

"By solving four riddles," said Morgan. She reached into the folds of her robe and pulled out a rolled-up paper.

"The first riddle is written on this ancient scroll," she said. "This book will help you to find the answer."

She held out a book. On the cover were the words *Ocean Guide*.

"This is where you have to go," said Morgan.

"The ocean! Oh, wow!" said Annie. She pointed at the cover. "I wish we—"

"Stop!" Jack grabbed Annie's hand. "How will we know if we've found the right answer to the riddle?" he asked Morgan.

"You will know," Morgan said mysteriously. "I promise you will know."

Jack let go of Annie's hand. She pointed again at the cover and finished her wish: "I wish we could go there."

The wind started to blow.

"Are you coming with us, Morgan?" Jack said.

Before Morgan could answer, the tree house started to spin.

Jack squeezed his eyes shut.

The tree house spun faster and faster.

Then everything was still.

Absolutely still.

Jack opened his eyes.

Morgan le Fay was gone.

Only the ancient scroll and the ocean book were left in her place.

2

The Reef

A breeze blew through the window.
Seagulls cried. Waves lapped the shore.

Annie picked up the riddle scroll. She
unrolled it. Together she and Jack read
the riddle:

Rough and grey as rock,
I'm plain as plain can be
But hidden deep inside
There's great beauty in me.
What am I?

"Let's find the answer," said Annie.

She and Jack looked out of the window. The tree house wasn't in a tree. It was on the ground.

"Why is the ground pink?" said Jack.

"I don't know," said Annie. "But I'm going out there."

"I'm going to do a little research first," said Jack.

Annie climbed out of the tree house.

Jack picked up the ocean book and flipped through it.

He found a picture of a pink island surrounded by water. He read:

This is a coral reef. Corals are tiny sea animals. After they die, their skeletons remain. Over time, the reef builds up from stacks of coral skeletons.

"Oh, wow, tiny skeletons," said Jack. He pulled out his notebook and wrote:

Millions of coral skeletons

"Jack! Jack! Come and look at this," cried Annie.

"What is it?"

"I don't know. But you'll love it!" she said.

Jack threw his notebook and the ocean book into his bag. He climbed out of the window.

"Is it the answer to the riddle?" he called.

"I don't think so. It doesn't look very plain," said Annie.

She was standing at the edge of the water. Beside her was a strange-looking machine.

Jack hurried over the bumpy coral to get a better look.

The machine was half on the reef and half in the clear blue water. It looked like a huge white bubble with a big window.

13

"Is it a special kind of boat?" asked Annie.

Jack found a picture of the machine in the ocean book. He read:

Scientists who study the ocean are called oceanographers. Sometimes they travel in small diving vessels called submersibles, or "mini-subs," to study the ocean floor.

"It's a mini-sub," said Jack. He pulled out his notebook.

"Let's get inside it," said Annie.

"No!" said Jack. Actually, he did want to see what the sub looked like inside. But he shook his head. "We can't. It's not ours."

15

"Just a tiny peek," said Annie. "It might help us figure out the riddle."

Jack sighed. "OK. But we have to be careful. Don't touch anything," he said.

"Don't worry," said Annie.

"And take off your shoes so they won't get wet," said Jack.

He and Annie slipped off their shoes and socks and threw them towards the tree house.

Then they stepped carefully over the sharp coral.

Annie turned the handle on the hatch of the mini-sub. It opened.

She and Jack climbed inside. The hatch slammed shut.

The mini-sub was tiny. Two seats faced the big window. In front of the seats was a computer built into a control panel.

Annie sat down.

Jack opened the ocean book and read more on the mini-sub page:

Min-subs have strong hulls to keep air in and protect those aboard from water pressure. Computers are used to guide the mini-sub through the ocean.

"Whoops!" said Annie.

"What's wrong?" Jack looked up.

Annie was waving her hands in front of the computer. Now the screen showed a map.

"What's going on?" asked Jack.

"I only pressed a few keys—" said Annie.

"What? I said not to touch anything!" said Jack.

An air blower came on. The mini-sub jerked backwards.

"Get out!" said Jack.

He and Annie scrambled for the hatch. Jack grabbed the handle.

But they were too late.

The mini-sub slid off the reef.

Then it sank silently down into the deep.

3

Mini-Sub

"You've really done it now, Annie!" said Jack.

"Sorry, sorry. But look out of the window!" Annie said. "Look!"

"Forget it! We have to figure this out!" Jack stared at the computer. He saw a row of pictures at the top of the screen.

"What did you do?" he asked.

"I just pressed the ON button," said Annie. "The screen lit up. Then I pressed the starfish.'

"That must be the command to go

under the water," said Jack.

"Yes. Then the map came on," said
Annie.

"OK, OK. The map shows the reef,"
said Jack. "Look! There's the mini-sub on
the map! It's moving away from the reef."

"It's like a computer game," said
Annie. "I bet I know what to do."

Annie pressed a key with an arrow
pointing right. The mini-sub on the
screen moved right. The real mini-sub
turned to the right too.

"Great!" said Jack with relief. "You press the arrows to steer the mini-sub. So now we can go back."

"Oh, no, not straight away," said Annie. "It's so beautiful down here."

"We have to get back to the reef," said Jack. His eyes were still glued to the computer screen. "What if the owners find it gone?"

"Look out of the window," said Annie. "Just for one tiny second."

Jack sighed. He pushed his glasses into place and looked up. "Oh, wow," he said softly.

Outside the glass was a strange world of bright moving colour.

It looked like another planet.

The mini-sub was moving past red, yellow and blue coral – past little coral mountains, valleys and caves – past fishes of every colour and size.

"Can't we stay a little while? The answer to Morgan's riddle must be here," said Annie.

Jack nodded slowly. She might be right, he thought. Besides, when would they ever get to visit a place like this again?

4
Fish City

There were fish everywhere: floating over the swaying sea grass, eating on the white sandy bottom, peeping out of coral caves.

Some kinds of coral looked like blue fingers or lacy fans. Others looked like deer antlers or lettuce leaves or mushrooms or trees.

Jack read in the book:

Coral reefs are only found in warm, tropical waters. Nearly 5,000 different species of fish live around coral reefs in the Indian and Pacific Oceans.

Jack pulled out his pencil and notebook. He started to write a list.

Coral Reef Research

warm water
over 5,000 kinds of fish

"Look!" said Annie.
The sub floated past
a huge starfish. Then a
pink jellyfish.
Then a blue
sea horse.
Jack added to his list:

starfish
jellyfish
sea horses

"What is *that*?" said Annie.
Jack saw a creature that looked like a
giant pancake with a long tail.

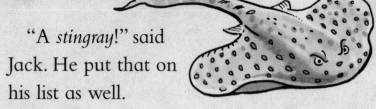

"A *stingray!*" said
Jack. He put that on
his list as well.

"And that?" said Annie.

She pointed at the biggest shell Jack
had ever seen. It was as big as a
footstool.

"I'll have to check on that one," said
Jack. He turned the pages of the ocean
book. When he got to the page about
clams, he read aloud. "The giant clam of
the coral reef is one metre wide and
weighs up to 200 kgs"

"Wow," said Annie.

"That's huge!" said Jack. He added
"giant clam" to his list.

"Dolphins!" cried Annie.

Jack looked up. Two dolphins were
peering through the window. They
tapped their noses against the glass.

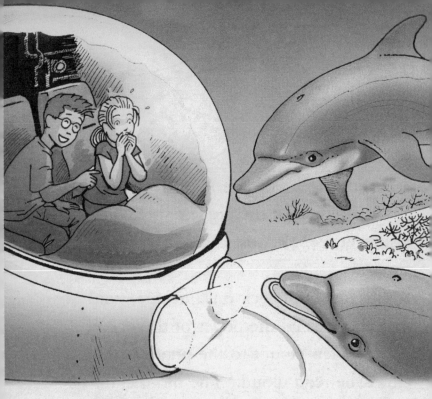

Their eyes were bright. They seemed to be smiling.

Jack laughed. "It's like *we're* in a fish tank – and they're looking at *us*," he said.

"Their names are Sukie and Sam," said Annie. "Sister and brother."

"You're crazy," said Jack.

"Here's a kiss for you, Sukie," Annie

said. She pressed her lips to the glass as if she were kissing the dolphin's nose.

"Oh, dear" said Jack.

But the dolphin opened her mouth and tossed her head. She seemed to be laughing.

"Oh, I know the answer to the riddle – dolphins!" said Annie. "They're grey and plain. But they have great beauty inside."

"You've forgotten the 'rough as a rock' part," said Jack. "Dolphin skin looks smooth and slippery."

"Oh, yes,' said Annie.

The dolphins flipped their tails. They swam off into the light-blue water.

"Wait! Don't go!" called Annie. "Sukie!"

But the dolphins were gone.

"It's time for us to go, too," said Jack. He was afraid someone might be looking for the mini-sub.

"But we haven't solved the riddle," said
Annie.

Jack studied the bright underwater
world.

"I can't see the answer," he said.
"There's nothing plain at all out there."

"Then maybe the answer's in the mini-
sub," said Annie.

They looked around the tiny space.

"I'll check the computer," said Jack. He
studied the row of pictures at the top of
the screen.

He pressed the book picture.

The words SHIP'S LOG flashed onto the
screen.

5

Two Eyes

"What's a ship's log?" said Annie.

"It's a diary of an ocean trip," said Jack.

He peered at the computer screen and read a log entry:

MONDAY 5TH JULY

"Hang on, that was just last week," said Jack. He read further:

COLLECTED ROCK AND SHELL SAMPLES

31

MAPPED OCEAN FLOOR
FOUND TINY CRACK IN HULL ·

"This is like your notebook," said Annie.

"Yes, the oceanographer was writing notes on the computer," said Jack.

Jack and Annie read further:

TUESDAY 6TH JULY
CRACK HAS WIDENED
MUST RETURN TO REEF SOON

"A crack *where*?" said Annie.

"I don't know," said Jack. He read further:

WEDNESDAY 7TH JULY
MORE TINY CRACKS
CANNOT BE FIXED
HEADING BACK TO REEF TODAY

"Uh-oh. This doesn't sound good," said Jack. He read further:

**THURSDAY 8TH JULY
DEFECTIVE SUB
RETURNED TO REEF
LEFT FOR HELICOPTER TO
TRANSPORT TO RUBBISH TIP**

"'Defective' means broken, doesn't it?" asked Annie.

"Yes," said Jack.

"So this sub is broken, isn't it?" Annie said.

"Yes," said Jack. "And it was waiting to be taken away by a helicopter. To a rubbish tip."

"Oh, dear," said Annie.

"Now we *really* have to get back," said Jack.

"Let's try
pressing the
waves picture,"
said Annie.

She pressed the
waves picture on the
computer screen.

The mini-sub began
to rise slowly.

"Oh, good," said Jack.

The sub went past a small coral
mountain. It went past schools of
fish and waving plants.

"Oh!" gasped Annie.

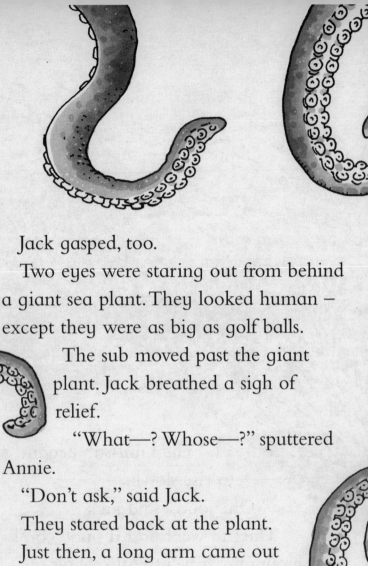

Jack gasped, too.

Two eyes were staring out from behind a giant sea plant. They looked human – except they were as big as golf balls.

The sub moved past the giant plant. Jack breathed a sigh of relief.

"What—? Whose—?" sputtered Annie.

"Don't ask," said Jack.

They stared back at the plant.

Just then, a long arm came out from behind it.

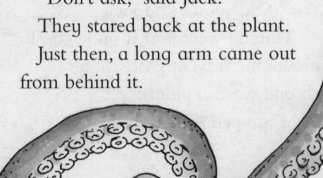

Then another arm came out.

Then another – and another – and
another – and another – and another –
and another!

Jack and Annie stared in
horror at a giant octopus.

"It's coming after us,"
said Annie.

Slowly, the octopus
crept through the water. Its
eight arms reached for the
mini-sub.

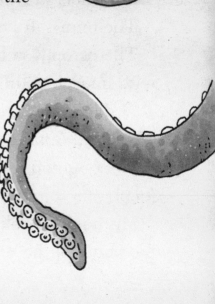

6

C-R-A-C-K

The octopus hugged the mini-sub. Each
of its eight arms had two rows of suckers.
The suckers stuck to the window.

The mini-sub stopped.

The octopus stared at Jack and Annie
with huge, human-like eyes.

"I don't think it wants to hurt us,"
whispered Annie. "It's just curious."

"I-I'm going to research it," said
Jack.

His hands shook as he flipped through
the pages of the ocean book.

He found a picture of an octopus and read out loud:

"The octopus tends to be a gentle, shy creature. Sometimes, though, curiosity gets the better of it and it comes out of hiding."

"Ah. See, I told you, he's shy," said Annie. She shouted to the octopus, "Hi! I'm Annie. He's Jack!"

"Oh, dear," moaned Jack. He read further:

"But the octopus has huge strength. Each of its arms, or tentacles, has many suckers, which act like rubber suction cups. It is nearly impossible to free an object from their grasp."

"Oh, great," said Jack. "We'll never get rid of this thing."

Just then, Jack felt a droplet hit his arm. Water. He looked up at the ceiling.

"Uh-oh," said Annie.

A thin crack ran along the ceiling. Smaller cracks branched out from it.

Water dripped from them.

"We've found the cracks," said Annie.

"The octopus had better let go! Before the whole ceiling breaks!" said Jack.

"Let go, *please*. Please!" Annie shouted at the octopus.

The creature blinked, as if trying to understand her.

"Please! Please! Please!" she shouted.

"Come on, Annie," said Jack. "It doesn't care if you're polite."

The octopus blinked at Jack.

"Get out of here!" Jack yelled at it. "Now! Go away! Shoo! Go!"

The octopus shot a cloud of black liquid into the water and disappeared into the dark cloud. Its long tentacles trailed through the water.

The mini-sub started to rise slowly again.

"You've hurt his feelings," Annie said.

"I don't think so . . ." Something bothered Jack. He looked back at the ocean book.

He read to himself:

The octopus squirts black ink to escape its enemies. One of its main enemies is the shark.

"Oh, no," said Jack.

"What's wrong?" asked Annie.

Jack looked out of the window. The water was growing clear again.

A shadowy figure moved towards the mini-sub.

"What is that?" whispered Annie.

The fish was way bigger than the dolphins. And it had a *very* strange head.

Jack could feel his heart nearly stopping.

"A hammerhead shark," he breathed. "We're *really* in trouble now."

7

Remain Calm

The shark swam behind the coral.

"Where did it go?" said Annie, peering out of the window.

"It doesn't matter," said Jack. "*We* have to get to the top."

"More water's coming in," said Annie.

"Yes, I know. Come on . . . come on . . . faster!" Jack ordered the mini-sub.

"Even *more* water's coming in," said Annie, "lots more!"

Jack looked up. The water wasn't dripping now – it was spurting.

"A few seconds, a few seconds," said Jack.

Suddenly, the mini-sub burst out of the water. It bobbed on the waves like a cork. The ocean sparkled all around it.

"Safe!" shouted Annie.

Jack felt the water rising around his bare feet.

"Hmm – not really . . ." he said.

"Whoops," said Annie. "The octopus must have made cracks in the bottom, too."

The water was up to their ankles now.

Jack looked out. He saw the reef in the distance.

"The sub can make it. It doesn't look that far," he said.

"Go, go, *go*," said Annie.

She pressed one of the steering keys.

Suddenly, the screen went blank.

"What's happening?" asked Jack.

Annie pressed the key again. Then Jack pressed the other pictures. Nothing happened.

"It's dead," said Annie.

"Oh, great," said Jack.

Now the water was up to their knees.

"I suppose we'll have to swim," said Jack. He took a deep breath.

"OK," said Annie. "It's a good thing we had swimming lessons this summer."

"Yes," said Jack. "And it's a bad thing we just saw a shark."

Jack quickly found the picture of the shark in the book.

He read out loud. "If you ever see a shark in the water, don't splash. Swim calmly away."

Jack closed the book.

"We'd better do the breast stroke," said Annie. "So we won't splash."

"Yes, and stay close," said Jack.

"*Very* close," said Annie. Her eyes were wide. But she seemed very calm.

Jack took a deep breath. He tried to be calm, too. He calmly took off his glasses. He calmly put them and the book into his bag. He calmly put his bag on his back.

Annie opened the hatch.

"Be calm," Annie said. She slipped out of the mini-sub.

"Help," Jack said calmly. He held his nose.

Then he calmly lowered himself into the ocean.

8

Swim for Your Life!

Jack moved his arms slowly. He moved his legs slowly. He gently pushed the water out of his way as he did the breast stroke.

Calm, calm, he told himself.

Annie swam beside him. They headed for the reef.

All was calm.

Then Jack saw something out of the corner of his eye.

A dark fin was zigzagging through the water. It was heading towards them.

Jack wanted to splash. He wanted to
yell. But he remembered: *calm*.

I'd better not tell Annie, he thought. *She'll
stay calmer if she doesn't know.*

He began to swim faster – then faster.
Annie went faster too.

They both swam as fast, and as
calmly, as they could.

Sometimes Annie went even faster than

Jack, which made *him* swim faster. And faster.

Jack was so scared that he wasn't tired at all. He was swimming for his life – and for Annie's life too.

He didn't look back to see if the shark was still there. He didn't want to know.

He just kept his eye on the tree house in the distance. And he kept swimming.

Jack and Annie swam and swam and swam.

It took forever for the tree house to get just a little closer.

Jack realized the reef was further away than he had thought.

He kept swimming, but his arms and legs felt heavy.

Annie was struggling too.

"Float!" she said. "Float!"

Jack and Annie turned onto their backs. They floated the way they had learned in their swimming lessons.

We'll just rest for a minute, Jack thought. *Then we'll keep going.*

But the more Jack floated, the more tired he felt. Soon he was too tired even to float. He started to sink.

Then he felt something.

His heart stopped. Something pushed

at him in the water.

It was slippery and alive.

Had the hammerhead caught up with them?

Jack closed his eyes and waited for the worst. He waited and waited. Finally, he opened his eyes.

In front of him was a shiny grey head – a dolphin's head!

The dolphin pushed Jack with its nose. It made happy clicking sounds.

"Hooray!" cried Annie.

Jack looked over at her.

She was clinging to the fin of another dolphin! Her dolphin was moving through the water.

Jack grabbed the fin of his dolphin.

Then the two dolphins swam smoothly through the water, pulling Jack and Annie towards the reef.

9

Ouch!

The sun shone on the ocean. It sparkled like a diamond.

Jack felt safe now. His dolphin was taking good care of him.

The dolphins slowed down as they neared the reef.

Jack lowered his feet. He felt the bumpy coral. He let go of the dolphin's fin and stood up in the water.

Annie stood too.

Then she threw her arms around her dolphin and gave her a big hug.

"Thank you, Sukie!" she cried. And she kissed the dolphin's nose.

Sukie tossed her head and clicked at Annie.

"Kiss Sam now!" Annie said to Jack.

"You're crazy," said Jack.

But Sam nuzzled Jack's head. Then he put his flippers around Jack's neck.

Jack couldn't resist. He threw his arms

around the dolphin and gave him a quick kiss.

Sam nodded and made clicking sounds like laughter. Then he turned to Sukie.

The two dolphins chattered to each other for a moment. They nodded at Jack and Annie and swam gracefully away.

"Bye, Sukie! Bye, Sam!" Annie shouted.

"Thanks!" Jack shouted.

The dolphins leaped high into the air. Then they dived back into the water with a SPLASH!

Jack and Annie laughed. "I wish we could swim like that," said Jack.

Jack and Annie watched the dolphins until they disappeared.

"I miss them already," Annie said softly.

"Me too," said Jack.

He sat down in the shallow water.

"I'm really tired," he said.

Annie sat beside him.

"Me too," she said.

The warm water lapped around their shorts and T-shirts.

Jack pulled off his bag. He took out his glasses and put them on. They were blurry with water.

"Guess what," said Annie.

"What?" said Jack.

"I saw the shark when we were swimming," Annie said. "But I didn't tell you. I wanted you to stay calm."

Jack stared at her. "I saw it too. I just swam faster so you would swim faster."

"And I swam faster so *you* would swim faster," said Annie.

"I guess we swam extra fast then," Jack

said. He shook his head with wonder.

"What now?" said Annie.

"We go home," said Jack.

"But we haven't solved Morgan's riddle yet," said Annie.

Jack sighed.

He pulled his notebook out of his bag. It was soaked.

He pulled out the ocean book. It was soaked too.

"We've failed," he said. "My research is all wet. We'll never be Master Librarians now."

Jack put everything away. "Let's go," he said sadly.

He stood up. Then he started across the pink reef towards the tree house. Annie followed him.

"Ouch!" Annie said.

"What's wrong?" Jack looked back.

"I stepped on something." Annie bent down to rub her foot.

"What?" said Jack. "A shell?"

"Yes, this . . ." She picked up a large grey shell and passed it to Jack. "Wow, it is rough. Rough and grey as a rock—"

"*And plain as plain can be!*" whispered Jack. They had found the answer.

The shell looked like a clamshell –
only bigger and with more ridges.

"How could *this* ugly shell be the
answer to the riddle?" said Annie. "What
about the part that says, 'There's great
beauty in me'?"

"Wait – research," said Jack. He
opened the soaked ocean book.

The pages were stuck together. But he
was able to turn a few.

He found a picture of the grey shell.
He read:

*Divers search for oysters in deep water.
But sometimes oysters wash up on reefs or
beaches. Inside some oysters you can find
a pearl. The pearl's natural beauty makes
it a treasure.*

"It must have a pearl inside it!" said Jack.

Annie peered into the crack between the two halves of the shell. "I can't see anything," she said. "How does a pearl get in there, anyway?"

Jack read out loud from the wet page:

"Sometimes a grain of sand will get between the oyster's shell and its skin. This irritates the oyster. So it makes a pearly material to surround the grain of sand. In this way, over a few years, a pearl is formed."

"I can't tell if there's a pearl in there or not," said Annie.

"Maybe we should bang it against a rock," said Jack.

"Now that would *really* irritate the oyster," said Annie.

"Yes."

"Maybe we should just leave it alone," said Annie.

She gently put the oyster back in the water.

"But how will we know if *oyster* is the right answer to the riddle?" said Jack.

"Morgan said we'd know," said Annie. "Come on."

Jack pushed his glasses into place. Then he and Annie picked up their shoes and socks.

They climbed through the window of the tree house.

Morgan's scroll was lying on the floor.

It was open.

"Look!" said Annie.

She and Jack stared at the scroll. The riddle had faded away.

In its place was one shimmering silver word:

OYSTER

"Morgan's magic," whispered Annie.

Jack let out a huge sigh. "We got it right," he said.

"And here's the Frog Valley book," said Annie. "Let's go home."

She opened the book. She pointed to a picture of the Frog Valley woods.

"I wish we could go there!" she said.

The wind started to blow.

The tree house started to spin.

The wind blew harder and harder.

Then everything was still.

Absolutely still.

10

The True Pearl

Dawn light slanted into the tree house.

No time at all had passed since they'd left. Day was breaking.

Jack rolled up the ancient scroll. He tucked it into the corner.

"We've solved the first riddle," he said. "Three more to go."

"I can't see another scroll," said Annie. "Maybe tomorrow we'll get the next riddle."

"That's OK," said Jack. "I think I need to rest — and dry out."

His T-shirt and shorts were still soaked. His rucksack too. Only his shoes and socks were dry.

"And this needs to dry out too," said Annie. She put the wet ocean book in a patch of sunlight.

Then Jack and Annie climbed down the ladder.

They walked through the woods, through leafy shadows and golden light.

They left the woods and turned down their street.

"You know, we should have found the answer to the riddle straight away," said Jack. "The oyster was on the reef all along."

"I know, but we wouldn't have had so much fun," said Annie.

"Fun?" said Jack. "You call being squeezed by an octopus and chased by a shark *fun*?"

"Don't forget the dolphins," Annie said simply.

Jack smiled. "True," he said. The dolphins made up for everything. *They* were fun.

"I guess they were the *true* pearl in the oyster," said Annie.

"Yes . . ." said Jack. "I wonder what Sam is doing right now."

"Sam?" Annie grinned at him. "You're crazy," she said.

They climbed their steps and went into their house.

"We're back!" Annie shouted.

"Did you get your shoes wet?" their mum called.

"Not at all," called Jack. Then he and Annie slipped up the stairs to change their clothes.

Magic Tree House™

By MARY POPE OSBORNE

"Beautifully written, full of suspense
and well researched"

Waterstones Books Quarterly

"A fast-paced and exciting
read which will appeal to
both boys and girls"

Junior

COLLECT THEM ALL!

www.**magictreehouse**.co.uk

Mary Pope Osborne is the author of over forty books for young people, including novels, picture books, biographies, mysteries, and retellings of fairy tales and myths. She was president of the Author's Guild, the leading organization for professional writers in the US for two years and has won many awards for her books. She lives in New York City with her husband, Will, and their dog, Bailey, who sleeps on top of Mary's desk every day while she writes.